Sammy the Snake

Mark Albini

Published in the United States of America

ISBN 978-1-962569-51-4 (SC)
ISBN 978-1-962730-95-2 (HC)

Mark Albini Publishing
155 weeping Willow Dr.,
Myrtle Beach South Carolina 29579
rhyminganimaladventures@yahoo.com.

Order Information and Rights Permission:

Quantity sales. Special discounts might be available on quantity purchases by corporations, associations, and others. For details, contact the publisher at the address above.

For Book Rights Adaptation and other Rights Permission.
Call us at toll-free 1-888-945-8513 or send us an email at
admin@stellarliterary.com.

Acknowledgements

A Special Thank You to my wife, Sharyn Albini, who had to listen to all the writes and rewrites over the years.

Dedicated to my parents, Louis Alfred Albini and Katherine Jeannine Albini.

Inspired by my love for animals, my love for America, my father Louis Albini, and Clement C. Moore.

Honoring my Christian Faith, my good friends and a few people from the past who were very special to me. I've used their names as the names of my characters in the Rescue Ranch Series. I had so many friends with the name Bob I had to use the name Bobo to cover them all. They became the voice of wisdom on the farm and it was a fun way to keep my friends around me. This way we could all live forever in the stories. I won't get them all in but I'm going to try.

The Creation of Rescue Ranch

It all began the day Grandpa Eddie purchased an old farmhouse that sat on a large parcel of land. The farmhouse was a few hundred miles from an old country zoo he used to visit as a boy. The zoo was closing after its caretaker had passed away but a family member stayed on to run the zoo until she could find a home for the animals. The Giraffes were chosen to be the first to go. Grandpa Eddie agreed to take the Giraffe family and drove up to the old farmhouse just in time to see the Giraffes arrive. They were dropped off in a field that backed up to an old red barn across the street from the house. Jimmy was excited to have a new home but surprised to find out he had to get up early. Tomorrow was a school day. On his way there he passed a shed with a beautiful white horse named Howie. Howie became Jimmy's best friend and on most days Jimmy would stop by in the morning and they would walk to school together. Some of the buildings they passed along the way had been rundown for years and it was obvious there was a lot to do on this old farm. Grandpa Eddie woke up early everyday of his life and went right to work. He needed to make room for some of the animals he was hoping to rescue. He planted some crops, cleaned out the barn and went looking for a hog to put in the sty. It didn't take long before it started to feel like home. He decided to call it The Rescue Ranch.

INTRODUCTION

The Rescue Ranch is a peaceful place where
animals live in wide open space.
They're fed everyday and have plenty to eat.
Life on this farm is really quite sweet.
It's a place for animals to come and stay and
meet new friends and have fun each day.
The animals are friendly and very sincere and
most have retired from a long career.
Except for those who were born on the farm and
a few in the woods that have caused alarm
If they live in the woods or somewhere on the farm
they all contribute to its countryside charm.
So welcome to the Rescue Ranch where
animals receive an olive branch.

BOOK #1   Jimmy the Giraffe
BOOK #2   Ricky the Rabbit
and Bobo the Mouse
BOOK #3   Terry the Turtle
and Freddie the Fish
BOOK #4   Sammy the Snake
BOOK #5   Phillip the Frog - - - COMING SOON!

RESCUE
RANCH

Sammy the Snake slithered home through the grass
after chasing a fish that played hooky from class.
It was Freddie the Fish and he got away
but it's a small pond and I'll see him someday.

I'll find him alone and sneak up from the back
and have Freddie the Fish for a dinner or snack.

I watched Jimmy, Howie and Bobo the Mouse
leave from the pond and walk towards their house.
Then Bobo the Mouse peeked out from the hay
and it made me feel hungry as I slithered away.

So I snuck through the grass and over a ridge
and headed for home to have a look in my fridge.

4

But when I arrived all I found was a treat
so I'll need to hunt something that's more filling to eat.

I went for a swim and I swam through the fog when I smelled something good. It was Phillip the Frog.

6

So I hid near a log lying still but awake
and waited for Phillip to jump in the lake.

But the frog didn't jump, he did not seem scared,
he hadn't seen me and I don't think he cared.
So I'm feeling quite sure that I'm going to be fed
unless Phillip grows eyes in the back of his head.

I climbed on the log and got ready to bite
when a blast from the past showed up to fight.
'Twas Terry the Turtle, a good friend to the frog
who came to warn Phillip about me on the log.

9

But then the log moved as the current got swift
and all I could see was Phillip adrift.

The log disappeared as it started to sink
and then a big eyeball gave me a wink.
'Twas Gary the Gator with a frog on his back
so I'll need to be smarter as I plan my attack.

Gary's eyes were afire as he stared straight at me
and that's why I panicked and decided to flee.

I was so scared facing off with that gator
that I had to leave and try something else later.
If Phillip sees me then he might be afraid
so I'll leave in the sun and circle back in the shade.

So I circled behind and I slithered on back
to make Phillip the Frog my next tasty snack.

But Terry the Turtle screamed "jump Phillip jump"
and the frog disappeared with a splash and a thump.

Phillip was gone and nowhere to be seen.
He dove to the bottom where the seaweed is green.

He blends in with the grass and it's so easy to hide
that I couldn't spot him as I looked side to side.

Now that Terry the Turtle helped my meal get away,
it's ruined my chance for an evening buffet.

18

I looked in my fridge when I went to my house
LIZARDS
MOUSE
19

And gave thanks to the Lord for some left over mouse.
MOUSE
20

Phillip the Frog had something to say.
He thanked his friend Terry for screaming that day.

And Gary the Gator just did his own thing.
When it comes to a lake the gator is king.
That's when Sammy the Snake got in the last word
and warned all the children of something absurd.
If you ever expect to have frog on the grill
you'll have to be smart and hunt with some skill.

So keep your eyes open wherever you go
and one day you'll learn how to hunt like a pro.
Or Gary the Gator will go on the hunt
and show you who is king and who is the runt.
So when you see something floating off through the fog;
watch out for gators and don't climb on a log.

www.ingramcontent.com/pod-product-compliance
Lightning Source LLC
Chambersburg PA
CBHW041145300726
48978CB00016B/1390